P9-ECU-423

Bright and Early Books

Bright and Early Books are an offspring of the world-famous Beginner Books® . . . designed for an even lower age group. Making ingenious use of humor, rhythm, and limited vocabulary, they will encourage even pre-schoolers to discover the delights of reading for themselves.

For other Bright and Early titles, see the back endpapers.

BRIGHT and EARLY BOOKS
for BEGINNING Beginners

for BEGINNING Beginners

BRIGHT and EARLY BOOKS
for BEGINNING Beginners

BRIGHT and EARLY B
for BEGINNING Beg

BRIGHT and EARLY BOOKS
for BEGINNING Beginners

and EARLY BOOKS
NNING Beginners

BR
for

BRIGHT and EARLY BOOKS
for BEGINNING Beginners

BRIGHT and EARLY BOOKS
for BEGINNING Beginners

BRIGHT and EARLY BOOK
for BEGINNING Beginner

BRIGHT and EARLY BOOKS
for BEGINNING Beginners

ARLY BOOKS
G Beginners

BRIGH
for BEG

BRIGHT and EARLY BOOKS
for BEGINNING Beginners

BRIGHT and EARLY BOOKS
for BEGINNING Beginners

BRIGHT and EARLY BOOKS
for BEGINNING Beginners

BRIGHT and EARLY BOOKS
for BEGINNING Beginners

BOOKS
eginners

BRIGHT and
for BEGINN

BRIGHT and EARLY BOOKS
for BEGINNING Beginners

BRIGHT and EARLY BOOKS
for BEGINNING Beginners

BRIGHT and EARLY BOOKS
for BEGINNING Beginners

BRIGHT and EARLY BOOKS
for BEGINNING Beginners

 Published in the United States by Random House Children's Books,
a division of Random House LLC, a Penguin Random House Company, New York.
Originally published in paperback by Random House Children's Books, New York,
in 1974.

Visit us on the Web!
randomhousekids.com

Educators and librarians, for a variety of teaching tools, visit us at
RHTeachersLibrarians.com

Library of Congress Cataloging-in-Publication Data
Eastman, P. D. (Philip D.)
The alphabet book / P. D. Eastman.
pages cm. — (A bright and early book ; [BE-41])
"Originally published in paperback by Random House Children's Books, New York,
in 1974"—Copyright page.
Summary: Such entries as American ants, birds on bikes, and cow in car present the
letters from A to Z.
ISBN 978-0-553-51111-6 (trade) — ISBN 978-0-375-97464-9 (lib. bdg.)
1. English language—Alphabet—Juvenile literature. [1. Alphabet.] I. Title.
PE1155.E27 2015 428.1—dc23 [E] 2014042161

Printed in the United States of America

10 9 8 7 6 5 4 3 2 1

Random House Children's Books supports the First Amendment and celebrates
the right to read.

ALPHABET BOOK

P. D. Eastman

A Bright and Early Book
From BEGINNER BOOKS®
A Division of Random House

A

American ants

A B C D E F G H I J K L M N O P Q R S T U V W X Y Z

A B C D E F G H I J K L M N O P Q R S T U V W X Y Z

B

Bird on bike

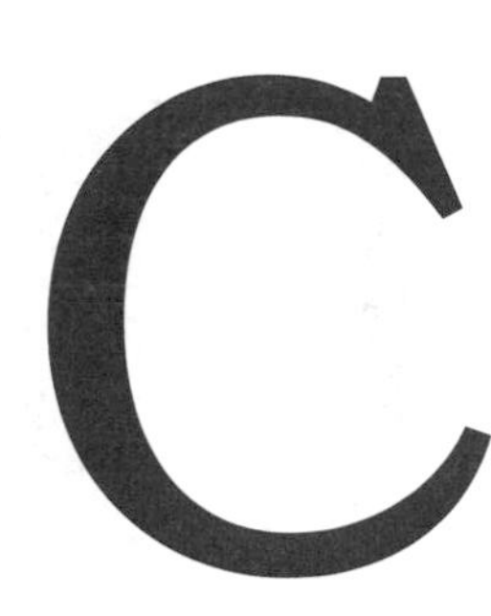

Cow in car

A B C D E F G H I J K L M N O P Q R S T U V W X Y Z

A
B
C
D
E
F
G
H
I
J
K
L
M
N
O
P
Q
R
S
T
U
V
W
X
Y
Z

D

Dog with drum

E

Elephant on eggs

A B C D E F G H I J K L M N O P Q R S T U V W X Y Z

F

Fox with fish

G

Goose with guitar

A
B
C
D
E
F
G
H
I
J
K
L
M
N
O
P
Q
R
S
T
U
V
W
X
Y
Z

A
B
C
D
E
F
G
H
I
J
K
L
M
N
O
P
Q
R
S
T
U
V
W
X
Y
Z

H

Horse on house

I

Infant with ice cream

A
B
C
D
E
F
G
H
I
J
K
L
M
N
O
P
Q
R
S
T
U
V
W
X
Y
Z

A
B
C
D
E
F
G
H
I
J
K
L
M
N
O
P
Q
R
S
T
U
V
W
X
Y
Z

J

Juggler with jack-o'-lanterns

Kangaroos with keys

A B C D E F G H I J K L M N O P Q R S T U V W X Y Z

A
B
C
D
E
F
G
H
I
J
K
L
M
N
O
P
Q
R
S
T
U
V
W
X
Y
Z

L

Lion with lamb

M

Mouse with mask

N

Nine in their nests

O

Octopus with oars

A
B
C
D
E
F
G
H
I
J
K
L
M
N
O
P
Q
R
S
T
U
V
W
X
Y
Z

A
B
C
D
E
F
G
H
I
J
K
L
M
N
O
P
Q
R
S
T
U
V
W
X
Y
Z

P

Penguins in parachutes

Q

Queen with quarter

A B C D E F G H I J K L M N O P Q R S T U V W X Y Z

A
B
C
D
E
F
G
H
I
J
K
L
M
N
O
P
Q
R
S
T
U
V
W
X
Y
Z

R

Rabbit on roller skates

S

Skunk on scooter

T

Turtle at typewriter

U

Umpire under umbrella

A
B
C
D
E
F
G
H
I
J
K
L
M
N
O
P
Q
R
S
T
U
V
W
X
Y
Z

V

Vulture with violin

W

Walrus with wig

A B C D E F G H I J K L M N O P Q R S T U V W X Y Z

Xylophone for Xmas

A B C D E F G H I J K L M N O P Q R S T U V W X Y Z

Y

Yak with yo-yo

Z

Zebra with zither

A
B
C
D
E
F
G
H
I
J
K
L
M
N
O
P
Q
R
S
T
U
V
W
X
Y
Z

BRIGHT and EARLY BOOKS
for BEGINNING Beginners

BooKs
inners

BRIGHT and EA
for BEGINNING

BRIGHT and EARLY BOOKS
for BEGINNING Beginners

IGHT and EARLY BooKs
BEGINNING Beginners

BRIGHT and EARLY BOOKS
for BEGINNING Beginners

BRIGHT and EARLY BOOKS
for BEGINNING Beginners

Ks
s

BRIGHT and EARLY
for BEGINNING Be

BRIGHT and EARLY BOOKS
for BEGINNING Beginners

T and EARLY BooKs
GINNING Beginners

BRIGHT and EARLY BOOKS
for BEGINNING Beginners

BRIGHT and EARLY BOOKS
for BEGINNING Beginners

BRIGHT and EARLY Boo
for BEGINNING Beginne

BRIGHT and EARLY BOOKS
for BEGINNING Beginners

EARLY BooKs
ING Beginners

BRIG
for BE

BRIGHT and EARLY BOOKS
for BEGINNING Beginners

BRIGHT and EARLY BOOKS
for BEGINNING Beginners

BRIGHT and EARLY BOOKS
for BEGINNING Beginners

BRIGHT and EARLY BOOKS
for BEGINNING Beginners

LY BooKs